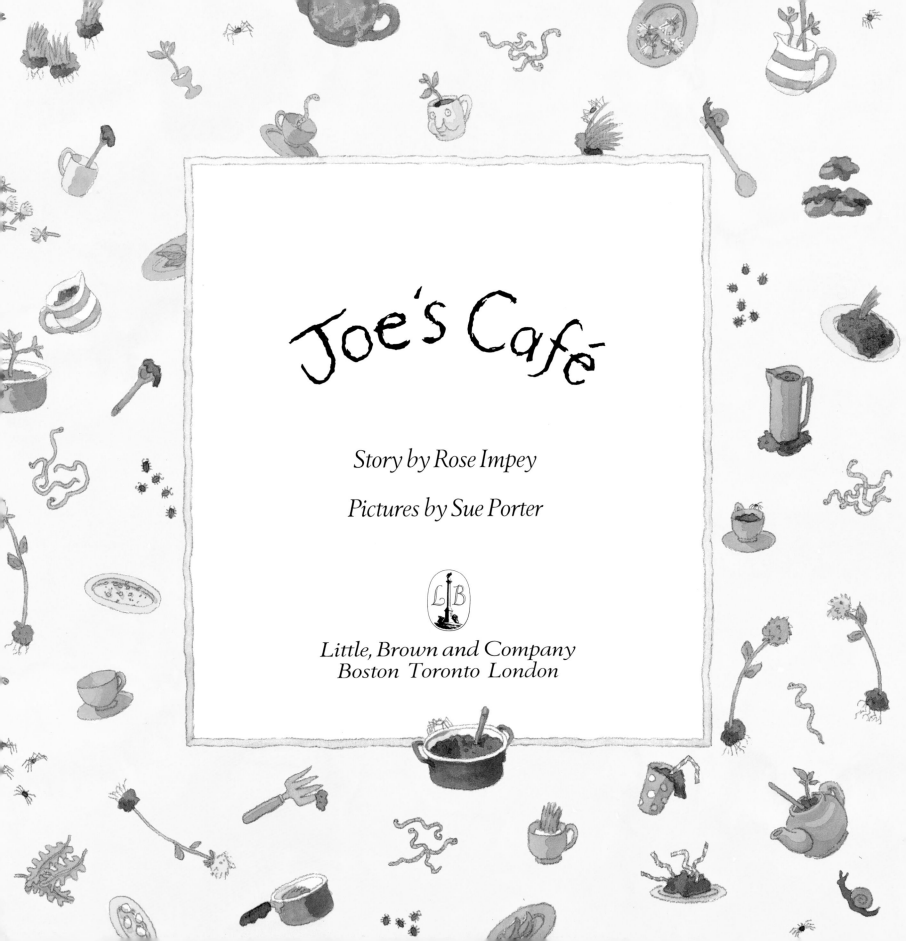

Joe's Café

Story by Rose Impey

Pictures by Sue Porter

Little, Brown and Company
Boston Toronto London

For my brother Graham,
who got lost

Text copyright © 1990 by Rose Impey
Illustrations copyright © 1990 by Sue Porter

First North American Edition 1991

First published in Great Britain in 1990 by Orchard Books, 96
Leonard Street, London EC2A 4RH

Library of Congress Cataloging-in-Publication Data
Impey, Rose.
    Joe's cafe/story by Rose Impey: pictures by Sue Porter. — 1st U.S. ed.
    p.   cm
    Summary: Big brother Joe comes to understand what the
responsibility of being in charge means when his little sister
disappears while Joe is playing a game.

ISBN 0-316-41777-7

    [1. Brothers and sisters — Fiction. 2. Play — Fiction]
1. Porter, Sue. ill. Title.
PZ7. 1344 Jo 1991
[E] — dc20   90—40466

        10 9 8 7 6 5 4 3 2 1

Published simultaneously in Canada
by Little, Brown & Company (Canada) Limited

Printed in Hong Kong

It was a hot, sunny day and Mom was busy baking.
She said to Joe, "Take Amy out in the backyard for me like
a good boy. I won't be long." She put on Amy's sun hat.
"Now, remember," she said, "Joe's in charge."

Joe groaned. He did love his
little sister, but the trouble was
Amy was too small to play
any of Joe's games.

She couldn't play pirates on the jungle gym.
She kept on falling into the sea.
"Watch out! The sharks'll get you,"
Joe told her. But Amy didn't
know about sharks.

She couldn't play going to the doctor. She wouldn't lie down and pretend to be sick. Amy spent too much time lying down in real life.

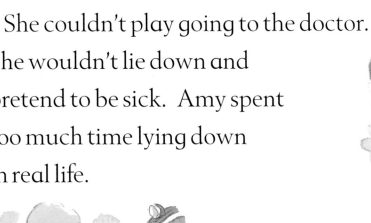

She was more interested in how Dad's bike worked.

"Oh, Amy! Look at you," said Joe.

And she couldn't play Joe's favorite game either — Creepy Crawly Café.

"You can't *really* eat them," said Joe. "Just pretend."

In fact, the only game Amy liked to play was hide-and-seek. She loved secret places where she could sit, sucking her thumb, hiding, until Joe came to find her.

She hid in all sorts of places:

behind the wheelbarrow,

in the flowerbed,

under the laundry.

When Joe found her he said,
"Oh, there you are."

"Boo!" said Amy, and she laughed as if it was a real game. Then the minute Joe turned his back, off she went again.

Joe began to feel hot and grouchy. He didn't want to spend the afternoon searching for Amy.

"You're a pain and I'm tired of you," he told her.

After that Joe went back to his café and Amy had to wait a very long time to be found.

Dad had dug a hole at the end of the lawn to make a sandbox
for them. It wasn't finished yet so there was no sand, but Joe
had smoothed out a comfy place to sit where the dirt
was soft and easy to dig. He made a hole, poured in the water,
and stirred it with an old wooden spoon. He loved it when the
mud went slip, slop, slurp.

On the menu in Joe's café were lots of interesting dishes:

Joe's Café

worm pies and caterpillar Cakes

Mud flavored Milk Shakes

sloppy Spider stew

slug Sandwhiches

And, of course, plenty of plain mud pies.

Sometimes Joe carried his mud pies to the front gate to see if there were any customers passing by.

Today it was very quiet in the road but soon he saw Mrs. Griffiths, who lived at the farm, walking home from the bus.

"Would you like to come to my café?" Joe called to her.

"I was just thinking about a cup of coffee," said Mrs. Griffiths, "and perhaps a muffin."

"I've got some delicious Snail Cookies," said Joe.

"My favorite," said Mrs. Griffiths.

He handed her a bucket and a plastic plate. And then Joe passed lots of other things for her to try, until all his dishes were lined up outside in the road.

"Mmmm, I feel much better now," said Mrs. Griffiths. "How much do I owe you?"

"Errm, ten cents," said Joe.

"What a cheap café," she said. "I'll come here again." She gave Joe a shiny new *quarter.* "You can keep the change." Then she smiled and waved goodbye.

Joe kept opening his fist and looking at the money shining in the sun. Quickly he opened the gate to pick up his dishes. He took them back to his café, so that he could make some more food to sell.

While Joe had been busy selling milkshakes and cookies, Amy had found
a new secret place to hide — right in the middle of the lilac bush.
It was cool and cozy, with the smell of lilac around her. She waited
for ages, crushing the lilac flowers between her fingers.

But this time Joe never came. He had completely forgotten about
Amy; he had forgotton he was in charge. And now because he was
excited — and because his hands were full — Joe forgot another very
important thing: to close the front gate. Leaving it wide open, he
walked back along the path, sat down in the dirt, and started to dig.

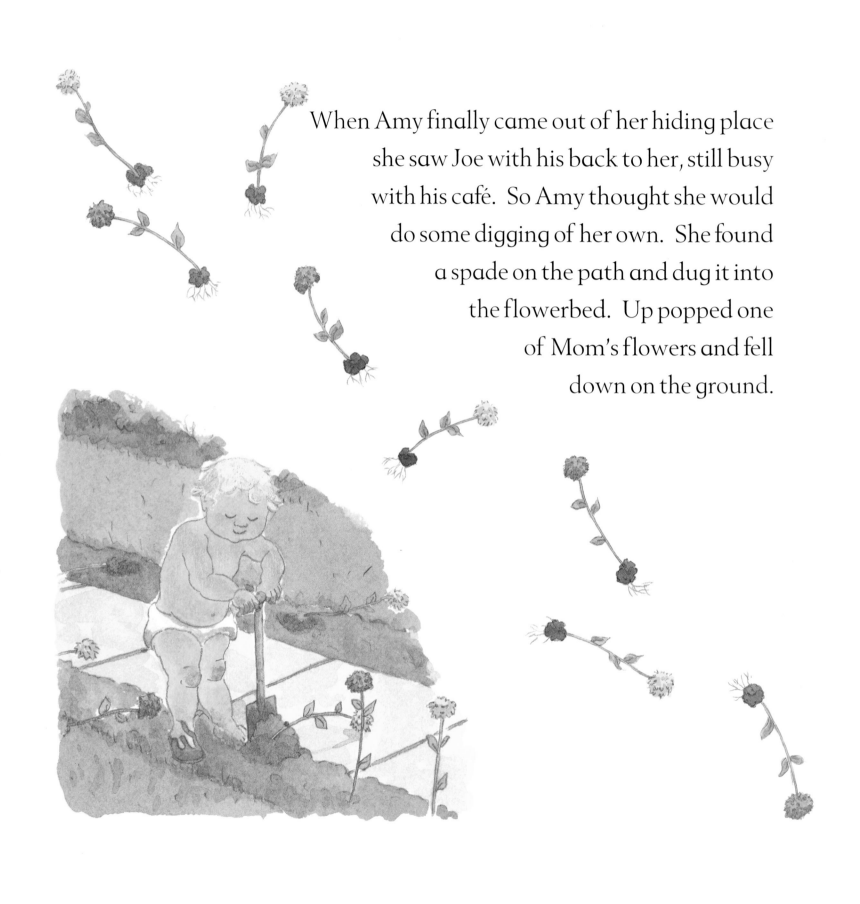

When Amy finally came out of her hiding place
she saw Joe with his back to her, still busy
with his café. So Amy thought she would
do some digging of her own. She found
a spade on the path and dug it into
the flowerbed. Up popped one
of Mom's flowers and fell
down on the ground.

Amy laughed. "All fall down," she said. She dug up another one, and another, and a few more along the path, until she came to the front gate. When she saw it wide open Amy smiled. And then, because she was just a baby and there was no one to stop her, Amy kept on walking, out into the road, dragging the spade behind her. Off she went, wearing only a diaper.

It was much later when Joe missed her. He suddenly noticed how quiet it was. He looked for her in all the usual places:

under the wheelbarrow,

in the flowerbeds,

behind the trash can,

under the laundry.

But Amy was nowhere to be seen.

Soon Joe noticed Mom's flowers lying on the ground. He followed the trail to the front gate — *which was still wide open.* Then Joe knew what had happened and, what's more, Joe knew it was his fault.

He stepped out into the street. It was quiet and still. The sun beat down on the pavement and on Joe's head. He looked up the street, which led to the main road. He hoped Amy hadn't gone that way.

He looked down the street, which led to the farm. Maybe she had
gone that way. But how could he know? There was no one to ask.
Joe didn't know what to do next.

 He knew what he should have done. He should have run straight into the house and told Mom. But Joe didn't do that because he had been left in charge. He wanted to find Amy himself before Mom realized she was gone.

Joe wasn't allowed out in the street, but he ran quickly to the first house. He went up the path and knocked hard on the door.

No one came. The house was silent and empty. Joe tried the next one and the next, but they too seemed to stare at him, without answering. By the time Joe reached the last house he was feeling scared. He'd never been this far — all by himself.

At last someone did answer.

Mr. Garner opened his door, rubbing his eyes.

"Have you seen Amy?" Joe asked him. "I've lost her."

But Mr. Garner had been taking a nap.

He hadn't seen anyone.

"Does your mom know she's gone?"

Joe shook his head. His eyes filled with tears.

"I was supposed to be in charge."

"Don't worry," said Mr. Garner, "she can't have gone far on those little legs. You wait while I put my shoes on, then I'll help you find her."

Joe sat on a stone by the gate at the end of the street. The tears ran down his face. He felt someone's hot breath on him. It was Bella, Mr. Garner's dog. Joe stroked her and rested his head against hers.

"I've lost Amy," he whispered, as if the dog might be able to tell him where to look. But Bella just panted and wagged her tail.
Joe had never felt more unhappy in his life.

 Then, through his tears, he saw Bella slip under the gate. She began to bark. Joe climbed up onto the gate to see why. In the distance someone was waving. It was Mrs. Griffiths, and by the hand she was leading a small figure wearing only a diaper.

"Mr. Garner!" Joe called. "I've found her!"

He climbed over the gate and ran as fast as he could to meet them. When he reached Amy he hugged her and squeezed her until she could hardly breathe.

"I do love you," he whispered. "And you're not a pain."

But Amy waved him away with a sticky hand, clutching a large chocolate cookie. "Wait till Mom sees your face," said Joe. There was chocolate all over it.

Joe pulled up Amy's diaper, which by now was almost around her knees, and took her other hand.

He would have liked to carry Amy, but after her adventure Amy felt far too grown up for that.

They said goodbye to Mrs. Griffiths, then Joe and Amy walked slowly back along the path to where Joe could see Mom waiting with Mr. Garner by the gate. He knew what she would say. "Oh, Joe, how could you?"

The tears came at once. "I'm really sorry," he said. And Mom could see he was. She felt too relieved to be angry. She gave him a hug.

"What we need now," she said, "is a glass of lemonade."

"You could come to my café," said Joe. "I'll make you some Beetle Soda."

Mom smiled. "Why don't you come to my café instead?" she said. "I've finished all my baking."

And since it was such a beautiful, sunny day Joe said, "We could have a picnic, in the garden. Just you and me ... and Amy."